St.

A Peach Street Mudders Story

All-Star Fever

by Matt Christopher

Illustrated by Anna Dewdney

Little, Brown and Company

Boston   New York   Toronto   London

To Nicholas Lee and Kyle Lee Christopher

First Paperback Edition

Library of Congress Cataloging-in-Publication Data

Christopher, Matt.
    All-Star fever : a Peach Street Mudders story / by Matt
Christopher ; illustrated by Anna Dewdney. — 1st ed.
        p.   cm.
    Summary: Bus Mercer, shortstop for the Peach Street Mud-
ders, wants desperately to be picked for the county All-Star
team, but he breaks his parents' rules for riding his new bike,
and feelings of guilt affect his game.
    ISBN 0-316-14265-4 (hc)
    ISBN 0-316-14198-4 (pb)
    [1. Baseball — Fiction. 2. Guilt — Fiction.]
I. Dewdney, Anna, ill.   II. Title.
PZ7.C458A1   1995
[Fic] — dc20   94-34184

10 9 8 7 6 5 4 3 2 1

*Published simultaneously in Canada
by Little, Brown & Company (Canada) Limited*

PRINTED IN THE UNITED STATES OF AMERICA

1

"Steee-rike!" boomed the umpire.

Bus Mercer took the call without batting an eye. After all, the first two pitches Bucky Neal had thrown had been balls. The Green Dragons' pitcher had already walked one man this inning, the fourth in the game. There was only one out. Bus figured he could afford to take a strike call.

The next pitch was another ball. Bus relaxed, feeling sure that Bucky would walk him, too.

Then Bucky breezed in a belt-high pitch that caught Bus off guard.

"Steee-rike!"

Bus stepped quickly out of the box. As he ran his hands up and down the aluminum bat, he glanced over at the stands. Sitting somewhere in that crowd of Peach Street Mudders fans were scouts for the county All-Star team. Bus knew they were watching every player who came to bat, every player who fielded a ball. The best ones would be chosen to play in the All-Star game coming up in two weeks. It was a game every kid in the league would give his right arm for. Well, almost.

Bus knew he had to make this next pitch count if he was going to stand a chance of making that special team.

"Belt it, Bus!" Rudy Calhoun yelled from the on-deck circle.

Bus stepped back into the box. He swung hard at the next pitch. A high-hopping grounder toward short! Dropping the bat, he beat it for first base. But the shortstop fielded the ball and winged it to the first baseman in plenty of time.

Drat! Bus thought sourly. *I really needed that hit! Instead, I just made a stupid out.* Then he remembered Coach Parker's warning before the game.

"Those scouts will be watching this team for three games. So if you miss out on one play in one game, don't dwell on it. Just make a mental note to try a bit harder next time, then put the play out of your head. Nothing hurts a player's concentration more than worrying about something that can't be changed. A good attitude is as important as a good play — and those scouts will be looking for both."

So Bus tried to shake off his disappointment by joining the bench in cheering on the next batter.

But Rudy Calhoun, the Peach Street Mud-

ders' catcher, struck out on four pitches to end the fourth inning.

"C'mon you guys! Let's stop 'em again!" Coach Parker yelled, clapping his hands as the Mudders took to the field for the beginning of the fifth inning.

The Mudders looked neat in their white, blue-trimmed uniforms, a sharp contrast to the green, white-trimmed uniforms the Dragons wore.

Bus got into his position, covering the hole between second and third, and joined in the infield chatter. "C'mon Sparrow! Get 'em outta there! Make it one, two, three!"

Smack!

A streaking grass-cutter shot past Sparrow's legs for a single.

But that was the only hit the Dragons got that inning. A fly-out, a ground-out, and a strikeout ended their turn at bat.

"Okay, Sparrow," Bus called as the pitcher tossed off his glove and picked up a bat.

"We've got to get onto that scoreboard to win this one! Show 'em you can hit as well as you pitch!"

Sparrow did. He laced a line drive over second base for a single. The bench stood up and joined the Mudders fans in a loud cheer.

Then Barry McGee doubled, advancing Sparrow to third. But Turtleneck Jones and José Mendez both popped out. It looked like Sparrow and Barry might die on base. With two outs and the game still scoreless, T.V. Adams stepped to the plate. Bus held his breath as the ball left Bucky Neal's hand.

T.V. came through with flying colors. He belted a sky-reaching fly ball to deep left field that went for a triple. Both Sparrow and Barry made it home. The score was now Mudders 2, Dragons 0.

Nicky Chong flied out to end the inning.

As Bus jogged onto the field, he half hoped the Dragons would get some hits this inning. He wanted the Mudders to win the game, but he wanted to show the All-Star scouts what he could do in the field, too. And if the Dragons scored enough runs to tie the game, the Mudders would come to bat in the bottom of the sixth inning. Then Bus would get another chance to bat.

Bus grit his teeth. *I'm ready,* he thought with determination.

2

The Dragons came to the plate looking ready to spit fire. It was the top of the sixth and final inning, their last chance to score.

And score they did. A sizzling single between first and second was followed by a high-flying homer over José Mendez's glove. The score now read Mudders 2, Dragons 2.

Bus pounded his fist into his glove. *C'mon, hit it to me!* he thought.

Beans Malone did just that. He drilled a hot, grass-hugging grounder directly at Bus.

Bus saw the ball moving toward him like the head of a snake. Never had a ball come at him so fast.

He put his glove down between his legs. But to his horror, the ball zipped right through and continued on into the outfield!

Bus scrambled to recover it, but it was too late. Beans Malone stood grinning on second base. Bus had blown his chance to impress the All-Star scouts again.

Fortunately the Dragons' next three batters got out one, two, three. The score remained tied at two runs apiece.

Bus was the second batter up for the Mudders. He selected his bat and walked to the on-deck circle. Barry McGee sidled up beside him.

"You should've had that grounder," he said. "Didn't anyone ever tell you to keep your tailgate down? Way down?"

"Cut it, Barry," T.V. Adams said. "That

was a hard-hit ball. If Bus *had* stopped it, it would have carried him to the outfield!"

Thanks, T.V., Bus wanted to say. He thought about the coach's warning again, but it was hard to shrug off Barry's hurtful words.

Alfie had made it to first. Bus took a few practice swings and stepped into the box.

I've got to try to hit him home! he thought.

Then he saw Coach Parker signaling him to bunt.

No! Bus wanted to scream.

The first two pitches were wild. The third pitch came in at chest level, Bus's favorite kind. He didn't think. He just swung as hard as he could.

Crack!

A line drive right at the pitcher! Bus dropped the bat and ran as hard as he could to first. But the pitcher had fielded the ball and thrown it to second in time to get Alfie out. Then, like a well-oiled machine, the Dragons' second baseman threw to first.

Bus just wasn't fast enough to beat that throw. In a booming voice, the umpire called him out. He had caused a double play!

The coach called him over. "Bus, a good bunt could have advanced Alfie safely to second even though it might have gotten you out. Next time, follow my signal."

Bus hung his head and nodded. The dugout was silent as he took his seat among his teammates.

Bus felt sick. He tried to cheer when first Rudy, then Sparrow got on base. He tried to join in the excitement when Barry hit a home run to change the final score to Mudders 5, Dragons 2. But he just couldn't. All he could think about was how he had probably ruined his chances to make the All-Star team.

3

After the game, Bus picked up his glove and started for home. He'd only walked a block when he heard someone calling his name.

"Bus! Bus, wait up!"

T.V. Adams rode toward him on his mountain bike. Bus looked at the bike with envy. It was just what he had asked for for his birthday last month. But instead, his parents had given him a new glove and some books. He liked his gifts, but he couldn't help being disappointed all the same.

T.V. patted him on the shoulder. "Hey, Bus, don't worry about that double play. It could have happened to anyone. Besides, we won the game, didn't we?"

"I should've paid attention to the coach's signal," Bus mumbled. "First an error in the field, then a double play. Looks like you'll be sitting on the All-Star bench without me."

"Oh, yeah? Well, I predict you'll show those scouts a thing or two in the next game!" T.V. said with a sly grin. Bus had to grin back. T.V.'s "predictions" were legendary, especially when it came to baseball. He'd even been accused of spying once because he always seemed to know things other people didn't.

"I sure hope you're right this time, T.V.," Bus said with a sigh.

"Besides," T.V. continued, "remember what Coach Parker said: No sense in dwelling on things you can't change." T.V. thought for a moment. "Think he means we *should* dwell on things we *can* change?"

"But if we knew what we should change, we'd just do it, wouldn't we?" Bus pointed out.

"Guess it would depend on what needed changing," T.V. mused.

When Bus walked into his kitchen a few minutes later, his mood brightened. His father was cooking up his world-famous spaghetti and meatballs for dinner. Bus wasted no time changing into fresh clothes and joining his parents at the table.

"Is it a special occasion?" he asked, helping himself to the pasta.

"How'd you guess?" Mr. Mercer asked. He winked at Mrs. Mercer. She winked back.

Bus was perplexed. "What's going on?" he wondered.

"Oh, nothing too important. Just a little belated birthday 'something' waiting for you in the garage. But first," she added as Bus leapt to his feet, "you have to finish your dinner."

Bus groaned and slid back into his chair. After what seemed like hours, he held up his clean plate for inspection.

"What, don't you want dessert first?" his father joked.

Bus rushed out to the garage without bothering to answer. When he flicked on the lights, he couldn't believe his eyes. There, in the corner by the lawn mower, stood a brand-new mountain bike! The card on the handlebars read "For Bus, with much love from Mom and Dad."

"Wow!" Bus yelled. He turned to see his parents standing in the doorway. "It's great!"

"We wanted to give it to you on your real birthday, but the bike store didn't have the right one for you. We had to wait until they got more," Mrs. Mercer explained. "Better late than never, though! Happy birthday, Bus!"

Mr. Mercer looked at Bus seriously.

"There are a few ground rules that go along with this bike, Bus. Rules that you must obey or else we'll have to take the bike away from you. First, always wear your helmet. Second, follow the rules of safety and use hand signals. And third and most important, always let us know when and where you're going riding. Deal?"

"Deal!" Bus agreed.

"One last thing," his mother added. "Stay on the town bike trails and side streets whenever possible. It may take you a little longer to get where you're going, but at least you'll be riding where it's safe. Besides, half the fun of riding somewhere is the riding itself, right?"

Bus nodded, his eyes shining. He was already mapping out his first bike route — to the baseball diamond for tomorrow's practice!

4

Bus felt like a king when he rode up to the dugout the next day. The Peach Street Mudders crowded around to admire his new bike. Then Coach Parker called for practice to begin.

Bus spent the next half hour shagging grounders, catching fly balls, and practicing his throws to first, second, third, and home. His fielding was good. Bus thought that if he could play so well during their next game, it would help his chances to make the All-Star team.

Then he took his turn at bat. He managed to hit a few sizzlers that shot past the infield's gloves, but he didn't get the grand-slam homer he was trying for. He was sure his chances of making the All-Star team depended on him making up for his two flubs at bat during the last game.

The sight of his new bike cheered him up. When practice was over, he strapped his glove onto the back carrier and adjusted his helmet so that it fit snugly on his head. He was about to head for home when T.V. called out to him.

"Hey, Bus! Want to go over to the batting cage?"

Bus hesitated for a moment. The batting cage was a fairly long ride from the baseball diamond. But he knew he could use the extra batting practice. And besides, hadn't his parents said going for long rides was what having a bike was all about?

"Sure, I'll come along," he said.

"Follow me! I know a good route that avoids the worst hills." T.V. buckled his helmet onto his head, hopped onto his bike, and pedaled off. Bus was close behind him.

The two boys stuck to the back roads that wound around the outskirts of town. Before too long, they arrived at the batting cage. They locked their bikes together, then paid a dollar each for a turn at bat. T.V. went first.

Pow! Pow! Pow!

T.V. hit his fourteen balls solidly one after another. Then Bus stepped into the cage for his turn.

Pow! Tic! Tic!

Bus hit all of his balls, but half of them went foul. *I've got to do better than this if I'm ever going to make the All-Star team!* he growled to himself.

He was fishing around in his pocket for another dollar when he felt the first raindrop. Only then did he notice that the sky had darkened with storm clouds.

"C'mon, let's get out of here!" T.V. yelled. A flash of lightning and a huge crack of thunder sent Bus and T.V. running for their bikes.

Big fat drops fell on the boys as they started pedaling toward home. Any minute the sky might open up and soak them completely.

"I know a shortcut," T.V. panted. "Follow me!" He veered off the bike path onto the main road.

Bus pulled up short. Suddenly his parents' rules echoed in his head. To his dismay, he realized he'd already broken one of them by not telling them he was riding to the batting cage. How could he break another one by biking on the main road?

T.V. braked to a stop. "What are you

waiting for? We're going to get drenched if you don't hurry up!"

"But what about the bike path? Can't we just take that instead?" Bus suggested hopefully.

"The bike path will take you ten minutes longer than my way! You can ride it if you want, but I'm not going to. I want me and my bike to stay dry!" T.V. looked at Bus impatiently. "Well?"

Bus glanced at the bike path one more time, then up at the dark sky. *I should get my bike out of the rain, too,* he thought.

He took a deep breath and cried, "Okay! Lead the way!"

5

The rain had really started to come down. Water splashed onto Bus's legs and passing cars honked their horns so loudly it made his heart hammer. He pedaled as hard as he could, but T.V. was faster. Bus could barely keep up. *Slow down, T.V.!* he wanted to cry.

Then T.V. disappeared around a corner. Bus was caught off guard. He had to pull sharply at his handlebars to make the turn. Wobbling off balance, he braked to a stop to catch his breath.

What he saw before him made his stomach flip-flop. He was staring down at one of the steepest hills he had ever seen. At the bottom, he could see cars zooming back and forth. T.V. was already halfway down that hill. Bus had no choice but to follow him.

Bus tested his brakes, then took a deep breath and started down the hill. Raindrops struck his face, but he coasted steadily downward. The traffic at the bottom loomed closer and closer. Bus tried to keep an eye on the pavement in front of him. He dodged one sewer grate after another. Finally a quick glance up told him he was almost safely at the bottom.

Wham!

His front wheel plunged into a pothole! Bus's teeth rattled and his hands bounced off the handlebars for a split second. He squeezed the brakes just in time to stop alongside T.V. at the busy intersection.

He had made it down safely. But somehow, all he could think of was what his parents would do when they found out.

Tired and soaked to the skin, he pedaled home and into the driveway just as the garage door opened up.

His mother and father were standing in the doorway.

"Bus! We've been worried sick about you! Practice was over an hour ago. Where have you been?" his mother asked with just a hint of anger in her voice.

"I — I was at the batting cage with T.V. We rode over right after practice," Bus replied.

"Without telling us? Bus, we asked you only last night to be sure to let us know where you were riding at all times!" His father frowned.

"I'm sorry. I guess — I guess I made a mistake," Bus whispered.

Mr. and Mrs. Mercer glanced at each other. Mrs. Mercer sighed. "Well, so long as

you're all right, I guess we can overlook it just this once. But if we find out you've disobeyed our rules again, we'll have to take the bike away from you until you prove you can be responsible. Now come inside and get out of those wet clothes and into a hot shower."

Bus followed his parents inside. Their kindness only made him feel more guilty. After all, he hadn't broken only one rule — he'd practically broken all of them!

What would his parents do if they found out? Even as he asked himself the question, Bus had a pretty good idea of the answer.

They would take his bike away, that's what they'd do.

But what if they didn't find out?

6

The next morning, Bus woke up with a headache. His mother insisted on taking his temperature. But Bus knew he wasn't sick. He just had had bad dreams all night.

Dreams of riding headlong down a hill that never ended. Dreams of his parents shaking their heads with disappointment while they wheeled his bike away. Dreams of every Peach Street Mudder but him wearing an All-Star uniform.

These dreams made Bus's stomach sink whenever he thought about them. He tried to push them out of his mind, but they just kept popping back in.

Two days later, the Peach Street Mudders were on the field again. This time, they were up against the Bay Street Stingers.

Bus carefully locked his bike to the bike stand and joined his teammates in the dugout. Coach Parker read off the roster:

"Turtleneck at first, Nicky at second, Bus at short, and T.V. at third. Outfielders left to right: Barry, José, and Alfie. Zero, you're on the mound, and Chess, you're catching for him. Jack, you and Tootsie stay warm and be ready to take over when needed. Okay, fellas, let's play a good game!"

Bus was surprised that the coach hadn't said anything about the All-Star scouts. He grabbed his glove to run out onto the field, but he turned back before he left the dugout. He had to know if the scouts were at the game.

"Yes, they are, Bus. They'll be watching this game and the next one, and then making their decisions," Coach Parker replied to his question. "But try not to think about them. Just concentrate on playing the best ball you can. That's all they need to see."

Bus nodded and ran to take his place at shortstop. He thumped his fist into his glove. It was his new glove, the one his parents had given him for his birthday. Just wearing it made him think about his other birthday present — and how he might lose it.

Why didn't I think before I took off yesterday? he thought miserably.

He snapped back to attention when he heard the umpire call for the start of the game.

Through the first four innings, the scoreboard was like a seesaw — first the Mudders were up and the Stingers were down, then the Stingers were up and the Mudders were down.

Bus made a few good saves and got on base twice, but during lulls in play, he found his mind wandering from the game. For some reason, he couldn't stop thinking about his parents' faces when they gave him the bike. They had seemed so happy, so proud of him.

What would their faces look like if they knew the truth?

At the end of the fourth inning, the score was tied at 3-3.

The top of the fifth inning started with a loud *crack* of a bat and the roar of the Stingers fans. The first batter, Frankie Newhouse, had made it safely to first.

Then the second batter, Henry Shaw, belted a high-bouncing grounder just to the right of shortstop. Bus took a step to the side, caught it, and whipped it to second.

The throw was high! Too high! It sailed over Nicky's head. Henry made it to first base and Frankie to second — all thanks to Bus's error!

Bus turned and headed for his position at the edge of the grass. His stomach felt as if it were loaded with rocks. *Nicky should've caught it,* he thought. *He hardly jumped a foot.*

But deep inside he knew differently. It would have taken a six-footer to catch that throw.

Put it out of your mind, he thought angrily. *Concentrate! No more mistakes!*

Mistakes seem to be all you can make lately, a voice inside him seemed to say. Bus gritted his teeth and shook his head.

The Stingers' pitcher was up next. He drilled Zero's second pitch over T.V.'s head. Frankie made it home, edging the Stingers ahead, 4-3, but Henry played it safe. He stood up at third.

The next batter smashed a mile-high drive to center. José staggered underneath it, and Bus shut his eyes for a moment, afraid José would miss it.

He didn't. One out.

Zero Ford threw two strikes on the next Stinger before the batter belted a chest-high pitch to deep left. It sailed over the fence for a home run. The Stingers now had a solid lead, with 7 runs to the Mudders' 3.

That was the best they could do that inning, though.

Alfie Maples led off the Mudders' turn at bat with a walk. Bus was kneeling in the on-deck circle, thinking about the dumb throw he had made. If he had made it good, the Mudders might not be four runs behind. And the scouts —

"Bus!" T.V.'s shout startled Bus. "What're you waiting for? You're up!"

Bus sprang to his feet and trotted to the plate. His mind hadn't caught up with his body yet when the first pitch breezed in.

"Steee-rike!" boomed the umpire.

The next three were balls. Then the pitcher delivered a streaking fastball level with Bus's knees. Bus slammed it over short for a single. Alfie stopped on second.

The hit made him feel a little better. Maybe the scouts would consider the hit more than they would the bad throw. After all, you had to get on base before you could score runs. And scoring runs was what this game was all about.

Just as this thought crossed Bus's mind, he happened to glance into the stands. What he saw there made his heart grow cold.

His parents were sitting with Mr. and Mrs. Adams. What if T.V.'s parents told his parents about their ride down the hill? If they did, then Mr. and Mrs. Mercer would know he hadn't told them the truth — and his new bike would be as good as gone!

A sudden shout interrupted his thoughts.

"Run, Bus, run!" the first-base coach was yelling at him desperately.

To Bus's horror, he saw Chess running down the first baseline toward him. Chess had gotten a hit and was trying to beat the throw to first — and Bus was just standing there like a dope!

Bus spun and started to run toward second as fast as he could. Behind him, he heard the ball smack into the first baseman's glove, then the umpire's call: "Out!"

Then he heard the first-base coach yell, "Slide!" He hit the dirt and felt his foot touch the base just as the ball landed with a thud in the second baseman's out-held glove.

"Out!" the umpire yelled.

7

Bus felt sick. Never had he made such a foolish error before. If only he had been paying attention, he might be standing on base, cheering on the next batter!

Alfie was still on base when Barry "Hit-Away Kid" McGee stepped to the plate.

Pow!

The Mudders fans let out a cheer as Barry blasted one over the fence for a home run! The score now read Stingers 7, Mudders 5.

Then Turtleneck flied out and the teams switched places.

The Stingers couldn't change the score during their turn at bat. They got out one, two, three. Bus helped by making a dead-on throw to first that was caught a split second before the runner tagged up. But the cheers of the crowd did little to lift his spirits.

The Mudders prepared to take their last raps at bat. They were only down by one, so they still had a chance to take the win.

Bus watched José take a few practice swings, then knock one into deep center that the Stinger fielder caught easily. One down.

T.V. sliced a line drive through the hole between first and second for a single. Then Nicky followed with a high fly ball that the shortstop bobbled. T.V. slid safely into second and Nicky made it to first. Alfie Maples stepped to the plate, and Bus moved into the on-deck circle.

But he never got his turn at bat. Alfie hit a

dribbling grounder that the second baseman fielded easily. He stepped on second, then relayed it to first for a double play. The final score read: Stingers 7, Mudders 5.

Bus shook hands with the other team along with the other Mudders, but all he wanted to do was get his gear and head for home. He had played badly, probably costing the team the game. No one said anything to him as he left the dugout.

His parents caught up to him as he unlocked his bike. In silence, they walked home, Bus wheeling his bike at his side.

One last chance, Bus thought. *The scouts will be at one more game.*

Bus gripped the bike's handlebars and stole a guilty glance at his parents. And how many more chances would *they* give him if they found out the whole truth?

8

The sun shone bright and warm the following Saturday. It was a perfect day for a baseball game. And, Bus decided, it was the perfect day to come clean about what had happened the day of the storm.

I've had it with sleepless nights! he said to himself.

But when he wandered into his mother's office to confess, he found her on the phone. Bus waited patiently for five minutes. Ten.

Fifteen. Finally, just as his mother hung up, Bus looked at the clock.

"Yikes!" he yelled. "I didn't realize it was so late! Bye, Mom!" He ran out to the garage.

Hurriedly he strapped his glove to his bike rack and made sure it was secure. Then he reached up to his handlebars to unhook his helmet straps.

But his helmet was gone! The handlebars were empty!

Bus was dumbfounded. He looked all around the bike. Nothing. He dug through the big wooden box that held his basketball, roller skates, and other sports stuff. Nothing. He even looked in his father's tool chest. Nothing.

Bus banged through the door to the house and charged upstairs to his room. *Maybe I brought it up with me last night,* he thought hopefully. But a quick look around his room showed that the helmet wasn't there, either.

There wasn't enough time for Bus to walk or run over to the baseball diamond. He had to take his bike. But when his parents had given him the bike, they had warned him never to go riding without his helmet. They had also warned him to take care of his equipment, and that included his bike helmet. If he rode over to the game without finding his helmet first, he'd be disobeying two rules!

But Bus knew there was nothing Coach Parker hated more than tardy players. If he didn't make it to the warm-up on time, he might have to sit on the bench for the first few innings. That was no way to impress the All-Star scouts!

Bus knew he had two choices. He could make it to the game on time by riding without his helmet — or he could confess to his mother that he had misplaced it and hope that she would understand.

Bus walked straight into his mother's office.

When she saw him standing there, she said, "I'll call you right back" and hung up the phone.

"What's wrong, Bus?" she asked quietly.

Bus hung his head. "I — I can't find my helmet. I know it's my job to take care of my bike and my equipment, and I'm sure I left it on my handlebars like I always do! But it's not there, so I guess — I guess I lost it somewhere, and you'll have to take my bike away," he finished lamely.

But when he looked up, his mother was smiling at him. She opened a drawer in her desk, reached inside — and pulled out his helmet!

"Where did you find it?" Bus cried happily. He quickly fit it onto his head and snapped the buckles under his chin.

"I have a confession to make, too, Bus,"

his mother said. "I took your helmet and hid it."

Bus stared.

"The Adamses told us about your little ride in the rainstorm. When we found out you had disobeyed us so badly and then lied to us, too, we almost took your bike away then and there. But you've never deceived us before, Bus, so your father and I decided to test you. Would you disobey our rules again if you had the opportunity?" She thumped him on top of his head. "I guess this answers our question."

Mrs. Mercer stood up. "Now, get yourself on that bike and get over to your game! Those Mudders need their number one shortstop to win against the Stockade Bulls!"

9

When Bus pedaled out of the driveway, he was grinning from ear to ear. His parents had given him a fright when they hid his helmet. But he guessed it was only fair. After all, he had frightened them when he didn't come home right after practice that stormy day!

Bus turned onto the bike path that wound its way past the backyards of many houses in different neighborhoods. If he hadn't been in such a hurry, he would have enjoyed the way the sun shone through the trees and maybe stopped to watch a squirrel carry an acorn to its hiding place.

But he was in a hurry. He had to get to that game on time!

Bus pedaled furiously, harder than he ever had. The paths were all familiar now, and he sped along smoothly.

Bowowowowowow!

A flash of brown leapt into the path in front of Bus's bike. Bus didn't have time to veer to one side. With a cry, he toppled over and landed in a heap. His head struck the pavement and he saw stars. To make matters worse, something wet and slimy was licking his face.

Bus struggled to sit up. With a grunt, he pushed away the big brown dog. "Silly mutt," he muttered. The dog barked a few more times, then sat down and looked at Bus — and the bike.

The sight that met Bus's eyes made his

heart sink. The frame and the wheels were fine, but his chain had fallen off. Bus had no idea how to fix it. He could have cried.

"Hey, kid, are you okay? Waldo! Waldo, come here, boy!"

Both Bus and the dog looked up at the sound of the man's voice. It was the dog's owner. Waldo jumped up happily, tail wagging. Bus just sat on the pavement. He was going to be late to the game now for sure.

"Kid, are you okay?" The man knelt down beside Bus, looking closely into his eyes.

Bus nodded. "I'm okay, but my bike isn't," Bus said sadly. "And I absolutely have to make it to my baseball game on time!" The man helped him to his feet and picked up his bike.

"Is that so? Well, it's a good thing you were wearing your helmet, or you might not have made this game or any other!" the man said. "Now, don't you worry. I've fixed a few bike chains in my time. While I fix yours, why don't you tell me about your team and why it's so important you make it there on time."

So Bus told the man all about the All-Star scouts and his hopes of playing on that special team. He told him about how his parents had tested him, too — and how he had passed. As he did, he suddenly realized that he felt happier than he had in days.

Why is that? he wondered to himself.

A few minutes later, the bike was as good as new. Bus's hopes soared.

"Thanks a lot, mister!" he said. He climbed onto the bike. "I'm sorry, but I have to get going."

"Hold on just one second more, Bus, and let me write a note for you to give Coach Parker. Maybe he'll understand." The man took a notebook out of his breast pocket and scribbled something. Then he tore the paper off, folded it in half and handed it to Bus. "You just see that Coach Parker reads that before he decides who's going to be playing at shortstop today, okay?"

"Okay!" said Bus. He stuffed the note into his pocket and sped away. "Thanks again!" he called over his shoulder.

It wasn't until he saw the baseball diamond up ahead that something strange occurred to him.

I never told that man my name. I wonder how he knew what it was? But he brushed the thought aside just as quickly as it had come to him. To his dismay, the Mudders were already running in from their warm-up in the field. If he was going to explain things to Coach Parker in time, he had to hurry!

10

Coach Parker read the note Bus handed him, then looked up.

"You sure you didn't get hurt in that fall, Bus? You know I can't play you if you're injured," the coach said.

Bus told him he felt fine. "I was wearing my helmet," he added.

The coach nodded his approval. "That's good, but it doesn't change the fact that you didn't make it here in time for the warm-up. Bus, I've already put Jack Livingston in the roster as shortstop. You'll have to sit out the first inning or two."

Bus's heart sank. No way he'd make the All-Star team now. Who would pick someone who was riding the pines, especially if that someone had made stupid mistakes in each of the past few games?

Then suddenly the coach's advice from the first game rang in his head.

"A good attitude is as important as a good play. Don't dwell on something you can't change — just try harder the next time."

Bus straightened up. The coach was right. Each game, each turn at bat, each ball hit your way was another chance to play the best ball you could. But to do that you had to *learn* from your past mistakes, not *worry* about them. Somehow, Bus had forgotten that. But he'd remembered it now.

The Mudders were on the field first, with Sparrow on the mound. His first pitches to the Stockade Bulls were sizzlers — two batters went down swinging. The third batter blasted a hot grounder to shortstop. Bus held his breath as Jack Livingston caught it on a high hop. But his throw to first was wild! The runner made it safely to first.

"C'mon, Jack, shake it off, shake it off!" Bus yelled along with the rest of the bench. Jack did. He made a beautiful play, covering second base when Nicky stepped off to field a ground ball hit between first and second.

The Mudders took their turn at bat, but by the end of the first inning the score still read Mudders 0, Bulls 0.

The second inning saw no change in the Bulls' score. But thanks to a single from Sparrow Fisher followed by a line drive from Barry McGee, the Mudders crossed home plate. Mudders 1, Bulls 0.

Bus was cheering for Turtleneck Jones when he heard Coach Parker call his name.

"Bus, grab a glove and warm up with Rudy. Jack, you've played a good couple of innings, but now it's Bus's turn."

Bus wasted no time. He and Rudy played catch for about ten minutes, watching first José, then T.V. get out at first. The inning ended when Nicky hit a pop fly that the pitcher caught.

Bus ran out onto the field, determined to make every play count. And he did just that.

His throws hit their mark every time. He remembered to "keep his tailgate down," as Coach Parker would say, when fielding grounders. He covered second and third base when Nicky and T.V. needed backup support. He even managed to make a double play by catching a line drive and throwing the runner out before he could get back to first.

And at bat, he concentrated on each pitch as never before. He was rewarded with two singles, plus a double that scored Alfie

Maples. By the end of the fifth inning, the Mudders had earned five runs. The Bulls had three.

The Bulls looked ready to change that score at the beginning of the sixth and last inning. The first batter socked a high fly ball to deep center field. José Mendez was just able to catch it before it could go sailing for a home run. One out.

"Okay, Sparrow! One down, two to go!" Bus yelled.

The second batter singled.

Then Sparrow threw three strikes for the second out. But the next batter blasted a double. Men on second and third, two out.

The crowd was shouting their encouragement to both teams as Sparrow let the next pitch fly. But their cheers couldn't drown out the sound of bat connecting with ball. A hard-hit baseball shot toward Bus. If he missed this catch, at least one man would score. Maybe two.

He had only a second to react. Up shot his glove. The ball hit so hard, it made the palm of his hand sting. But he had caught it!

The game ended with the score reading Mudders 5, Bulls 3.

Bus was congratulated by all his teammates and Coach Parker. He hadn't felt so good for a long time.

Only one thing can top this, he thought as he hopped on his bicycle to ride home. *And that would be getting a call from the All-Star scouts tonight!*

He had started to pedal away when he heard a loud *woof* from the stands. He looked up and saw two familiar faces grinning down at him. It was the brown dog and the man who had fixed his bike! The man waved but disappeared into the crowd before Bus had a chance to get near him.

I wonder who the heck he was, Bus thought. *Sure wish I could thank him again.*

Instead, Bus called out to T.V. to wait for him. Together, the two boys rode home.

It wasn't until later that night that Bus found out who the strange man was. He and his parents had just finished eating dinner when the doorbell rang. Bus answered it.

"Coach Parker! What are you doing here?" he asked.

Bus stepped aside to let Coach Parker and a second man in. He almost fell back in surprise when he saw who the second man was.

"Hello, Bus," the man said with a grin. "Bet you didn't expect to see me again."

Before Bus had a chance to answer, Coach Parker interrupted. "I think an introduction is in order. James Crandall, meet Bus Mercer. Bus Mercer, meet James Crandall — head scout for the county All-Star team."

Bus just stared, open-mouthed.

Bus's parents came into the room. "What's this all about?" his father asked.

"I wanted to talk to Bus face-to-face about the rosters for the All-Star team," Mr. Crandall said. He turned to Bus and laid a hand on his shoulder. "Bus, you're a fine shortstop. But I'm afraid there are two shortstops in the county who have better statistics than you. We had to choose those two players for the All-Star squad.

"However," he added before Bus had a chance to react, "you showed me something in today's game that impressed me. You showed you're not afraid to admit when you've made some mistakes, and you're willing to work to correct them. Bus, I would very much like for you to accept the position of substitute shortstop for the team."

Bus looked up, confused. "Substitute?"

Mr. Crandall explained, "If for some reason one of the other two shortstops couldn't play in a game or missed too many practices or something like that, you would play for the team in his or her place. As a substitute, you would practice with the team, get a uniform, and be at every game. Your name would be listed with all the other team members. You might even get a chance to play in one of the games. What do you say?"

Bus didn't even have to think about it. "When do we start?" he asked eagerly.

The four adults laughed. Then Coach Parker and Mr. Crandall said they had to be going.

After they left, Mr. and Mrs. Mercer gave Bus a big hug. "We're so proud of you, Bus. It's not every parent who has a good athlete *and* a good sport for a son."

Bus grinned. "And the best thing is, I have something to shoot for next year! Look out, All-Star team! Bus Mercer hasn't given up yet!"